SOMEBODY ELSE'S NUT TREE
AND OTHER
TALES FROM CHILDREN

SOMEBODY ELSE'S
NUT TREE

AND OTHER

TALES FROM CHILDREN

by Ruth Krauss

Pictures by Maurice Sendak

HARPER & BROTHERS   PUBLISHERS   NEW YORK

CONTENTS

The Happy Egg

There was a little little bird.
It was just born out of its mother
— still was an egg.
It couldn't sing.
It couldn't walk.
It couldn't fly.
It could just get sat on.
So it got sat on
and sat on
and sat on
and sat on
and sat on
and sat on
and sat on
and one day, POP! out it came
— could sing, could walk, could learn to fly
— could someday sit on other happy eggs.

There was a little girl who had always wished to be a queen.

So that night the Good Fairy came and asked, "What is your wish?"

And the little girl told her, "I wish to be a queen."

The Good Fairy granted the little girl's wish.

Next morning the little girl's mother came into the room and saw a little queen in the bed.

The mother screamed. "Help! Where is my little girl?"

The father came quick and he saw the little queen in the bed.

The father screamed. "Help! Where is my little girl?"

Then they both ran out of the house screaming. "Help! Where is our little girl? Police! Police!"

The little queen wished she was not the little queen.

Then the Good Fairy came and asked, "What is your wish?"

And the little queen told her, "I wish to be their little girl again because that is what my mother and my father wish. And besides the Police are coming. But I still wish to be a queen when I grow up."

So the Good Fairy granted the little queen's wish.

And when the mother and the father came running back into the house with the Police, they saw their own little girl in her own little bed. And everyone hugged her.

A Boy, a Woman, and a Cake

A boy went up in the air in a ship.
Then the ship broke
and he shot out
and he hit the ground and got hurt.
Then he went to the hospital.
And then he came home with all bandages.
And then his mother baked a cake for him.

Birth of the Daisies

Once nobody on earth could tell if their love
loved them
or loved them not.
Then a boy took a bit of sun
and sprinkled it around.
And very soon, up came some daisy-flowers,
with little yellow middles and little white rays,
looking like the big sun,
very pretty too, and just right for counting on their petals
loves me
loves me not.
And so the boy sat down
and picked a daisy-flower
and counted on its petals
— loves me
— loves me not
— loves me
— loves me not
— loves me
— loves me not
SHE LOVES ME

The Kitten and the Lion

There was a kitten.
And there was a lion.
And the lion chased the kitten
and the kitten ran.
She ran into the woods and dug a hole for the lion to fall in.
Pretty quick the lion came running after her
and he fell in the hole.
And he couldn't get out. He had to stay there.
Then Indians came and shot arrows in him.
And they killed him.
Then they shot arrows in all the lions on the world.
They killed all the lions on the world.
All the lions on the whole world died
and there never were more lions Evermore.
But there are still tigers.

A Girl at a Party

There was a girl at a party
and she was very beautiful.
Her face was beautiful.
Her dress was beautiful.
Her feet were beautiful.
Everybody said, "How beautiful!"
And she was rich too.
But the other girls at the party didn't care
because they all had warm bathrobes.

Once there was a little lost boy.

He was so lost nobody could even see him.

And he was cold too. He was in rags.

Now the more nobody saw him,

the more lost he got,

the more cold he got,

the more in rags he got.

Then, one day, somebody did see him.

First, she felt his shiver in the air.

Then, she heard his rags whipping him in the wind of the shiver.

And then, at last, she saw the boy.

"Oh!" she said. "How terrible to be so cold! Let me mend you."

"Yes," the little boy said.

So she took out her sewing basket and began to mend him.

He was so many rags, one spool of her thread was not enough.

So when her spool of white thread was gone, she began to mend in her
yellow thread. And when her yellow thread was gone, she began to mend
in the blue. And when the blue was gone, she began in the pink

and when the pink was gone she began in violet,

and then in red and in orange

and in purple and green—

all the colors in her basket she was mending in, which was practically
all the colors in the world.

And soon the little boy was very very whole again.

And he was warm again too in his coat of many colors.

Everyone could see him now. He was like a rainbow,

when the sun is shining through the rain.

And now there is this little found boy.

Happy Marbles!

A girl had one marble.
A boy came and played with her and he won.
Then she had no marbles.
There were plenty of marbles to buy
but the girl had no money to buy.
But the girl had a friend.
And the friend came and gave her a marble.
And then, the boy who had won away her first marble
came again and gave it back to her.
Now the girl has two marbles. She is VERY HAPPY.
She sings this song.
Happy marbles
Happy marbles
Happy marbles
to all —
Happy marbles
Happy marbles
Happy marbles
Hooray! to ALL

Once upon a long time ago, a Mr. and Mrs. Tree had a tree-baby.

"It's a girl!" they cried.

"And so delightfully different!" Mrs. Tree observed, bending over her little one. "We must name her a name as lovely and unusual as herself."

"We should maybe wait," Mr. Tree put in, "and see how she develops."

"Hunh!" a neighbor-tree whispered. "She certainly is different."

And "Hunh!" another neighbor whispered back. "Different is right! Prickly, I'd call it."

Now, time passed and the little one's first spring came. And, it happens, there was a fine Prince out wanting to be wooing, who seeing the forests so filled with the green of budding tree-girls, said to himself, said he, "I should take my time loving because a wedding is for keeps." So, all spring he took his time loving. The air was light and sweet.

He loved a fresh full maple tree. He loved a pale white dogwood.

He loved a weeping willow. He loved a fat and blooming apple.

Summer came. All summer he took his time loving.

He loved a thin tall poplar.

He loved a spreading chestnut tree.

"I am right to take my time loving," he said. "So many

beautiful tree-girls! And a wedding is for keeps."

Autumn came. And the trees grew more beautiful even than before. The wood was wild with yellows and reds and purples. All autumn the Prince took his time loving.

Winter came. And then, on the branches of the beautiful tree-lasses, the leaves of yellow and red and purple, the leaves that had once been green, shriveled and fell. The trees were bare. The trees were bleak. "I sure was right!" the Prince cried, "to take my time loving. Look, oh look, at the beauties now. I want a steady. Not one to come and go."

And then, before him suddenly, he saw a bright and shining young green thing, lovelier still among the dark ruins of his loves gone by.

"How beautiful you are!" he cried. "Who are you? For surely I never saw the like before! You are the one I would wed, if thou wilt have me. I took my time to find you, because a wedding is for keeps."

The young green tree just stood there. She gave no answer because she had no name to give.

"Speak to me," the Prince begged. "Tell me yes."

Then, "Yes," the little tree whispered. "But I cannot tell you my name."

At this moment her mother and father spoke out, calling, "Now we know your name, our little one. Your name is Evergreen. We name you Evergreen."

So the little tree told her Prince, "My name is Evergreen and yes, I said yes. I will thee wed."

And so they were. And their wedding was for keeps.

And all the children took after their mother, and their

children's children, and their children's children's children, right down to now.

And this is how young Evergreen brought happiness to herself, because surely it is happiness to marry your Prince. And she brought happiness to her Prince, because surely it is happiness to marry a happy girl. And she brought happiness to her mother and father, because now they had a protector with a shining sword. And happiness to us she brought, for all the steadfast trees of winter standing green and lovelier still among the goneby leaves of the year, now deep in the sleeping earth.

27

Birthday

There was a girl
and she had a cat
and a dog
and a chicken.
And she wanted a horse.
On her birthday
she got a horse.
And that day the horse had horses.

The White Boat

A great white boat came
crashing from the sky and hit the earth
— and the dirt flew up
and the rocks flew up
— the sky was rock and dirt
and rock and dirt was the sky
— the whole wide world exploded.
All the High-up people hid their eyes
— they should not see the sight of such sound.
They warned the children, "Hide your eyes!"
And the High-up Chief who never heard except inside,
lifted up his head
— and the earth was cracking open and the great white boat went
down in it. And at that spot a fountain rose, a spout,
and then it fell, and spread, and became a little sea-place
— and on it was a little white boat, just new, like a lily on a pond.
And now the people too lifted up their heads and looked
and all the children ran and looked
and the Chief made a journey out of himself and looked
down with his real eyes and saw, and said,
How beautiful is the little boat
— like a lily on a pond
— like a little white dream
on a sea of night,
how beautiful

There was once a girl out riding
— galoop galoop galoop galoop —
She wore her very good wedding dress.
She rode her very good silver horse.
She didn't know where she was going
but her horse knew where she was going.
Along came a man out riding too
— galoop galoop galoop galoop —
He saw the girl on the silver horse.
He saw her very good wedding dress.
He said, "Hello. I like you. I'll marry you."
So she told her horse, "Whoa-a!"
But he didn't whoa
— galoop galoop galoop galoop —
and she doesn't know where she's going
but her horse knows where she's going.
Then the man rides close and he says, "Whoa!"
He says, "Hey you! You behave now! You stop!"
And he takes the reins of the silver horse.
And the silver horse stops. And he whinnies.
Then, the man and the girl get married.
They hold hands
and they ride home
— galoop galoop galoop galoop
    galoop galoop galoop galoop —
together.

Rainbow Means Happiness

One time a little straw house was getting into a breeze.
And there was a big rainbow over it keeping the rains off.
But the rainbow cracked
and the storm broke down
and the little straw house was beat to sinking.
When then, some of the rainbow cracklings fell on it
and stuck in it
and made little happy-spots all over.
Part of the rainbow is part of the house now,
and part of the house is rainbow.

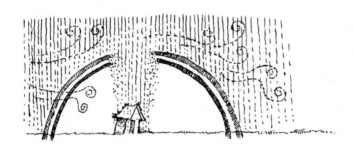

The Boy and the World

There was a boy who hugged the world and
the world hugged the boy and
the boy hugged the world and then
the world hugged the boy and then
the boy hugged the world again and then
the world hugged the boy again and then
the boy pushed the world away.
He said, "Go away, World!"
Then the boy hugged his mother and
his mother hugged her boy.

The Rain That Couldn't Rain

Once there was some rain in the sky.
But it couldn't rain.
The rain wouldn't let itself rain.
Then along came a big wind
and it had some hard rain in it.
And the hard rain hit
the rain that couldn't rain and
made it rain.
And then it rained
and it rained
and it rained
and it rained
Happy Everafter.

A Little Fish Story

Once there was a BIG fish.
And a little fish came swimming along.
And the little fish ate the BIG fish.
Then a little little fish ate the little fish.
And a little little little fish ate the little little fish.
And then a little little little little fish ate the
little little little fish that ate the
little little fish that ate the
little fish that ate the
BIG fish.
And they all went swimming along together.

Somebody Else's Nut Tree

In a big forest
was a little girl
and was a little nut tree
— a little pretty nut tree it was —
all alone.
So nobody could find it, the little girl thought.
But one day she came and she found it, she thought.
"Hooray!" she hollered. "I found a little nut tree."
And then,
she went close,
and she climbed it.
And she saw
it was somebody else's nut tree.